Two for Joy

Two for Joy

Gigi Amateau

illustrated by
Abigail Marble

CANDLEWICK PRESS

Text copyright © 2015 by Gigi Amateau
Illustrations copyright © 2015 by Abigail Marble

First edition 2015

Library of Congress Catalog Card Number 2014945701
ISBN 978-0-7636-3010-2

15 16 17 18 19 20 BVG 10 9 8 7 6 5 4 3 2 1

Printed in Berryville, VA, U.S.A.

This book was typeset in Scala.
The illustrations were done in graphite and ink.

Candlewick Press
99 Dover Street
Somerville, Massachusetts 02144

visit us at www.candlewick.com

To the unbreakable Audrey Ellis Gregg
and her great-granddaughter, Judith Ellen

G. A.

To Mom, who got me started, and to Ilene
and Elijah, who keep me going

A. M.

One

There I was, a starting forward in the biggest, most important soccer game of my Olympic career. With only a minute left, the game was tied. When my teammate made an awesome pass to me, the crowd began chanting my name: "Jenna! Jenna! Jenna!" I knew what I had to do. I looked up at the crowd and waved. I turned left, but there was nowhere to go. The other team had closed in all around me. They towered over me, but I was not afraid, not one bit. I pivoted right and barely squeaked through an opening that was just my size. I heard Mom in the *stands screaming her lungs out: "Good job, Jenna! Good job!" All the way down the field, I zigged and zagged and ducked and turned until there was nothing and no one left between me and the biggest, grizzliest goalie I had ever seen. I looked her right in the eyes and growled, "Look out—this one might hurt." I took a deep breath and kicked with all my might. The ball spun in midair. Then I heard a telephone ring and ring. The ringing grew louder and louder. Coach yelled, "Turn that phone off! Let's get back to the game!" But the phone kept right on butting into the game.*

I opened my eyes and looked around. There were no stadium lights, no roaring Olympic crowd, and no silky red-white-and-blue uniforms. I was wearing my green pj's with purple monkeys, but not my shin guards. My feet were bare. There were my cleats, right on the closet floor. Outside the window, the sky was still black and the stars were still bright. But the phone *was* ringing.

Who would call in the middle of the night?

A light crept under my door. Without making a peep, I tiptoed over the squeaky board in the hall and into Mom's room.

Mom was quiet on the phone and listening closely. I sat on the bed beside her and slipped my hand in hers. She squeezed my fingers and rubbed my hair, but didn't say a word. The house was so hushed, I could hear the refrigerator humming in the kitchen. I could hear a car passing down our street.

But I barely heard Mom say, "Thank you for calling." Then she hung up and turned to look at me.

"What's happened, Mama? What's wrong?"

Mom looked right into my face. "Here's the truth, my big girl. That was the hospital in

Pleasant Grove. Earlier tonight, Tannie fell. This time I'm really worried."

Tannie's our name for my great-aunt Britannia; she's just like me. There is nothing on earth that Tannie can't do. She drives a pickup truck as big as a barn. She goes to the races all by herself. One time she sang karaoke with Mom and me. She knows how to fly an airplane, and she has her very own motorcycle. She even played soccer a long time ago, way before it was cool.

Have you ever seen an old lady, like Tannie, head a soccer ball?

"What happened this time?" I asked Mom. "Did Tannie throw the lawn mower in the truck again?" The last time she did that, she had taken a nasty spill.

Mom shook her head.

"Did she slip off a tall ladder while painting

her house? Or fall from the tractor after cutting hay?"

Mom giggled a little, the way she does when she's nervous. She shook her head and sighed.

"No, no. This time it was none of those things," Mom tried to explain. "Tannie, as usual, was moving too fast. She missed a step off the back porch and has broken her ankle."

"Oh, that's it? She just fell off the porch?" was all I could think to say. Then finally I asked, "Will Tannie be okay?"

Mom looked worried, and she looked extra tired.

She answered, "Tannie is strong, but her bones have grown more fragile over the years. Her ankle will heal in time. She doesn't need surgery—that's the good news."

"Then, why are you so worried? My teacher broke her ankle and came right back to school, on crutches."

"It's not really Tannie's ankle that worries me; the fracture was stable."

My mom's a nurse, and sometimes she talks to me like I work at the hospital, too. I nodded and rubbed my chin as if I were the doctor. "Hmm, the fracture was stable," I repeated.

"Right. But this is the fourth time in half as many years that Tannie's fallen and hurt herself. I'm afraid it's only going to get worse," Mom said. "Next time it could be her hip or her back."

Then Mom added, "Tannie's doctor thinks the farm is too much for her now. It would be safer for her to live someplace smaller; she needs to be near people, not way out in the country, where no one is around to help. She's not going to like it, but Tannie needs to move."

I thought of Tannie's yard, full of pink tea roses and big, showy flowers like gladiolus and hollyhock. I pictured her vegetable garden, which spreads across an entire acre of land, so big it could be a soccer field. I remembered the bobwhite quail that I always flush out of the woods at Tannie's place. Tannie loves all kinds of birds, just like I do.

I've seen lots of birds in my life, but Tannie's seen lots more. Tannie keeps a list of all the different birds she's ever seen. She has hiked through mountains in Cuba to try to find a special woodpecker. She even flew to Peru to see the birds of Machu Picchu.

Almost 10,000 different bird species live on the earth! And my aunt Tannie has seen 3,026 of them. Now that I'm eight, I might just start a life list like Tannie's.

Then I remembered the chickens and the mean old rooster that run all around Tannie's farm.

"Where will the chickens go?" I asked. "What will she do?"

Two

Where else is there for Tannie to live?" I asked Mom.

"Don't worry about that now." Mom walked me back to my room. "Hop back in your bed, little one; find a good dream until morning." She pulled my Sunbonnet Sue quilt all the way up to my neck.

"Who made this quilt? Jenna Phoebe, do you remember?" Mom asked. She always uses both my names when she kisses me and tucks me in.

I snuggled in deeper. Yes, I remembered. "Tannie made it when she was my age. That was a long time ago, when she was a farm girl, with much stronger bones."

"This quilt has been keeping little girls warm for a lot of years," Mom reminded me. "First Tannie, then me, and now you." Mom kissed my nose good night.

"Try to get some sleep; it will be morning soon." The clock by my bed had flipped over to four o'clock; I flipped over to the left.

A mockingbird started singing like crazy right outside my window. I couldn't help but think of Tannie and her farm in Mississippi; there are lots of mockingbirds at Tannie's.

I fluffed up my pillow. I flopped to the right. I wished I could see Tannie soon.

I turned onto my back and then onto my tummy. No matter whether I curled up tight or straightened myself out, I could not get to sleep. That crazy bird would not stop singing.

I could only think of Tannie, my very most favorite aunt.

We're all the family Tannie has left in the world since her husband, Louis, died. I've heard stories about him; he's famous in my family. Everyone called him "Saint Louis" because he was such a good man and the only one with patience enough to handle Tannie's strong will. I never did get to meet Saint Louis; he died before I was born.

Now, other than the chickens, Tannie lives alone with her cat, Butt.

When we visit, Tannie's rooster acts like he is the boss of me. I have to be careful around him. Once, I tried to pet him, and he bit my finger. It didn't bleed, but it made me cry. The chickens are way nicer than that mean old rooster.

Tannie can make a chicken sound even better than a chicken: *"Bock-bock-bock-be-Gock! Bock-bock-bock-be-Gock!"*

Tannie loves those chickens like they are her babies. Maybe that's because she never had any babies of her own. I yawned. Actually, Butt is the biggest baby of all.

I yawned again and thought of how sweet Butt is to the chickens. Butt is so sweet, he even shows the rooster his tummy, and he never, ever lifts a paw to hurt the hens. Tannie says Butt is a pacifist—that means he loves peace.

Butt is the cutest cat I've ever seen. He's orange and white, with the sweetest pink nose and dainty little feet for a tomcat. He prances around Tannie's house, swishing his tail, always with his bottom high in the air—that's how he got his name.

He's also the smartest cat I've ever met. When Butt is thirsty for cool water, he takes

Tannie's finger in his mouth and pulls her to the sink. If Butt is hungry for a snack, he paws at the pantry. When it's too hot outside for yard work, Butt makes Tannie go inside. Ever since Saint Louis died, Butt has been Tannie's best friend.

I kicked the quilt away and dangled one foot off the bed. I wished I could blink twice and be at Tannie's farm.

I tried counting sheep, but the sheep turned into clucking chickens . . . and then a crowing rooster.

I closed my eyes to find my Olympic dream again. Instead, I dreamed of Tannie's fruit orchard, with strawberries in the spring, blueberries in the summer, and apples in the fall. I dreamed of how Tannie's chickens always let me reach under their soft, warm feathers to take enough fresh eggs for breakfast.

Where else could there be, besides the farm, for Tannie and Butt?

Three

Those dreamy chickens would have let me keep right on sleeping, but the high-whistling *weeeeeeet* of Mom's teakettle started calling for morning the way a rooster does while it's dark. I flipped over to my right and eyeballed the clock by my bed. Six o'clock! Roosters and teapots should learn to sleep late.

I pulled the covers back over my head, but the smell of biscuits in the oven came slinking up the stairs. *SST! SST! SST!* the sound of bacon went popping through the hall. Floppy bacon is my favorite.

And that mockingbird was still carrying on in the holly tree. If Tannie were here, she would say, "That bird has worked herself into a tizzy!"

Then, quick as anything, I remembered about Tannie's fragile bones. I hoped Tannie wasn't in too much pain. Mom says whenever I'm worried, I should sing to my guardian angel. (Just what you'd expect from somebody named Grace.) While I dressed for school, I made up an angel song for Tannie:

Go fast to Tannie; don't stop on the way,
Tell her I'm with her, all night and all day.
Help her get stronger,
Give her hugs and good care.

My guardian angel, I want you to share
A hug and kiss right on her face.
Tell her it's from us: Jenna and Grace.

When I finished my song, I blinked twice and sent my angel fast from our little yellow house in Virginia all the way to Tannie's big white farmhouse in Mississippi.

Today Mom didn't rush me or hurry me up. She didn't count down from ten or say, "Jenna, hop-to! The school bus will be here in seven minutes!"

Mom sat down and drank her coffee, while I ate all of the floppy bacon she made and three entire jelly biscuits. I wished we had a big breakfast like this every day. On most school days, I have plain oatmeal.

I sang my angel song for Mom. But I did not sing with my mouth full. Mom started to cry.

She wiped her eyes and said, "Teach your angel song to me, then we'll sing it together!"

Mom and I sang my song over and over, until we heard the school bus come rumbling down our street.

Mom looked at her watch. "Jenna, we're late."

VROOM-VROOM-VROOM! The living-room windows started to shake, the way they do when the bus rolls on past my stop.

"Gracious, we've missed the bus again."

I wrapped an extra biscuit in a napkin for later in the day.

On the way to school, Mom surprised me. "I've been thinking about something, and I'd like you to think about it, too. Jenna, we're all the family Tannie has left in the world. I'd like to ask Tannie to come live with us."

With us? I said to myself. *Awesome!* I thought. *Tannie and Butt will be with us all the time!*

"With us?" I said out loud. "Sweet! Tannie's coming to live with us!"

Mom kept right on talking. "I'll call a realtor and Tannie's doctor later this morning. We can take care of most everything next week on spring break. We'll go to Tannie's, instead of the beach, and bring Tannie back with us." Mom giggled again. "Is that okay?"

I love the beach, but I love Tannie more. "I don't mind, Mom. I'm worried about Tannie, too," I said.

We pulled up to school. Mom kissed me good-bye and told me, "We'll talk more at dinner. I love you, Jenna."

I told Mom bye-bye and raced off to class.

All day at school, I thought about Tannie coming to live with us. I remembered the taste of Tannie's buttery, sweet pound cake and hoped she would make it every day at our house. Then my teacher tapped my shoulder. "Jenna, are you with us? Pay attention, please."

I thought about my math facts, but only for a second.

Would Tannie like to have a tiny garden in our tiny yard? We could plant tomatoes and okra, squash and peppers.

My teacher called my name again. "Jenna! Where are you today?" I sat up straight and tall. I know my math facts better than anything.

I hoped Tannie would bring Butt, because I've always wanted a cat.

At recess, I didn't play soccer like usual. I stayed on the swings by myself and sang my angel song over and over. I wondered if my angel had made it to Tannie's place yet. I swung so high that everyone on the ground looked smaller, but not as small as they would look from a plane. I pumped my legs to go even higher. I imagined

what it would be like to swing all the way over the top. I bet Tannie did that once or twice.

The higher and higher I swung, the louder and louder I sang, until my teacher shouted, "Jenna, don't swing so high! Come down!" I was so high up, I could barely hear her.

I did what she asked, but I didn't stop thinking about Tannie and Butt coming to live with us.

Four

Mom and I got busy planning. We only had one week to get ready.

Mom talked to Tannie's doctor every single day, to be sure she had everything she needed to get better fast. We also called Tannie on the phone every morning and every night, just to check in and make sure she was fine.

Mom put the phone on speaker so we could all three talk together at once. I always got to talk first.

When I sang my angel song to Tannie, she

said my angel had actually already been there, but Tannie still liked my hugs and kisses best of all.

Then Mom tried to talk Tannie into moving with us.

But Tannie wouldn't agree. "We'll see what the doctor says next week when you come visit me. Grace, stop making such a fuss."

"I'm a nurse, Tannie," Mom said. "This is what I do. I take care of people."

Tannie told Mom she was making something out of nothing.

"When school is out next week, Aunt Britannia, we're coming to get you. We're going to bring you back with us. It's time for us all to be together." Mom added, "I won't take no for an answer." She hung up the phone and said to me, in a huff, "We're going to get ready for her, even if she isn't ready for us."

Mom looked around the kitchen. "I need to

make a 'Tannie List' of things to do to get ready."
She pulled a sheet of paper from the junk drawer.

I love making lists.

"I need to make a 'Tannie List,' too!" I said.
"May I have a sheet of paper?" Mom handed
me her paper and dug out an index card for
herself.

Mom's Tannie List:

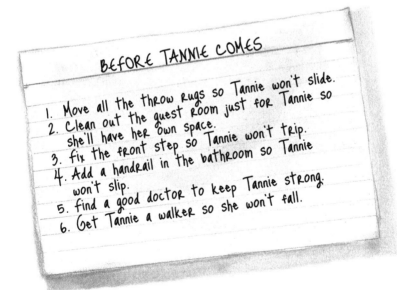

BEFORE TANNIE COMES

1. Move all the throw rugs so Tannie won't slide.
2. Clean out the guest room just for Tannie so
   she'll have her own space.
3. Fix the front step so Tannie won't trip.
4. Add a handrail in the bathroom so Tannie
   won't slip.
5. Find a good doctor to keep Tannie strong.
6. Get Tannie a walker so she won't fall.

My Tannie List:

AFTER TANNIE COMES

1. Build a tree house.
2. Dig a garden.
3. Hang bluebird boxes.
4. Make a cozy place for Butt in my room.
5. Bake pound cake every day.
6. Win a soccer game for Tannie.
7. Remember to ask for help sometimes.

Mom worked hard and stayed up late most nights trying to get everything on her list done. I went to school every day and mostly stayed up late helping Mom at night.

One more time, before we left for Mississippi, Mom asked Tannie to come live with us.

"Grace," Tannie told her, "let's see how I feel when you girls get here."

"That sounds like yes to me. We'll see you in a few days," Mom said.

We were ready to go get Tannie. *Would Tannie be ready for us?*

Five

On the day of our trip, we were supposed to leave before the sun came up, but Mom let us sleep in late again. She made floppy bacon and biscuits, too. We packed up the car fast. Before we hit the road, we went over the trip one more time.

"Jenna, it's a long drive to Tannie's. Do we have everything we'll need?" Mom asked me.

"I have thirty-three books and my old bunny, Hop," I said.

"I packed a cooler with ice and drinks," said Mom. "I've brought three bags of food, in case we get hungry."

"How about a map?" I asked Mom.

"No need for a map, sweet girl. I could make this trip driving backward. We'll go over the Blue Ridge Mountains and into Tennessee. Then we'll gain an hour by turning our clock back. We'll drive through the Great Smoky Mountains next. Once we're out of the mountains, we'll be almost there. Finally, after one time change, two mountain ranges, and three states, we'll see Tannie. If we don't dillydally this time, if we only stop when we need to, we'll be there before midnight, Tannie's time."

As we pulled out of the driveway, I waved good-bye to our house and to that noisy mockingbird, who was singing again in the holly outside my bedroom window.

"Good-bye, mockingbird! Wait until you get to meet Aunt Tannie next week! We're bringing her all the way back from Mississippi," I hollered out the car window.

Mississippi is so easy to spell. I learned to spell it when I was little, like this:

M–I

Crooked Letter–Crooked Letter–I

Crooked Letter–Crooked Letter–I

Humpback–Humpback–I

I spelled *Mississippi* over and over, until Mom asked me to stop. The whole entire day, we drove through Virginia. I read all of my books over and over again. I ate two ham sandwiches and three handfuls of chips. I looked out the window at the mountains.

"Are we out of Virginia yet?" I asked Mom.

"No, not yet, Miss Jenna. Virginia is a very long state, if you drive it sideways. Let's play a counting game to help pass the time," Mom suggested. "Hand me a pimento cheese sandwich, and I'll teach you how to play."

I dug out a sandwich for Mom.

"And some chips, too, please."

I dug out some chips for Mom and ate a couple more myself.

"Okay, Jenna, in this game, every time we see a church steeple, we have to sing the phrase *'Church bells do chime'* three times. You may sing high or low, fast or slow. The only rule is that you must sing it in a way that fits the church."

Virginia has a lot of churches. When I saw a sweet, little white church sitting atop a hill, I sang *"Church bells do chime"* fast and high, with lots of somersaults in my voice.

When Mom saw a fine brick church way down in a valley, she lowered her voice, deep like a man's, and said, "That is a very big, very

serious-looking church." She sang her song so slow and so low that it didn't sound like Mom. We sang and sang until we were hoarse.

When I got tired of singing, I still wasn't tired of counting, so I made up a new game.

"Let's count all the big trucks we see. And if we lose track, we have to start over; that's the only rule." All the way to two hundred thirteen or two hundred fourteen we counted. Then we got lost in our counting and had to start over. By the time we got to Tennessee, I was tired of trucks, but I still wasn't tired of counting.

"Let's count crows!" Mom said. "Like Tannie and I used to do when I was little. Saint Louis would drive us to Birmingham, and we'd tell our fortunes by the number of crows standing on the side of the road. Whoever sees a crow first starts counting like this: *'One for sorrow, two for joy, three for a girl, four for a boy, five for silver, six for gold, seven for a secret never told.'* I'll go first."

Counting crows sounded fun to me!

Mom saw one crow. "Uh-oh, one for sorrow. Too bad. I'll see more next time. Your turn next. Hey, do we have an apple left?" I handed Mom an apple and took one for myself.

"Two! I see two crows! One for sorrow, two for joy!" I shouted.

We took turns all through the Great Smoky Mountains. Mom always counted only one for sorrow for her fortune. I counted every number except seven.

"Look!" Mom said on her turn. "Three! Well, of course. Three for a girl and I have you."

We drove across the Tennessee River, and finally, on my turn, I counted seven crows.

"Wow, seven for a secret never told!" Mom slapped me a high five. "What do you think that means, Jenna? What is a secret never told?"

"Maybe, if there are diamonds buried in our

backyard, but nobody ever found them, not even in a million years."

"That's a good one," Mom said. "Or what if a unicorn lives way up in those Smokies, so deep in the forest that no person ever saw it and no one ever, ever knew that unicorns were real?"

Then I thought of Tannie and why we were making this trip. I wondered if Tannie had a secret never told. I whispered to Mom, "What if Tannie really does want to come live with us, but it's such a big, gigantic secret inside of her that she hasn't even told herself?"

"I think you've found our fortune, Jenna," Mom said. "Let's stop counting crows."

In Nashville, I stared out the window at the streetlights as they came on. Mom listened to the radio. I fluffed up my pillow against the window and rested my eyes.

The next thing I'll see will be Tannie, I thought.

Six

After fourteen hours—one whole day and most of a night—we turned into Tannie's drive at a quarter till midnight.

I ran to the house, straight to find Tannie. With her broken ankle in a cast, Tannie had to walk with crutches. She moved ever so slowly, but she and Butt were standing at the door waiting for us.

Tannie's hand shook a little when she reached out to me. "Jenna, let's get a good look at you."

Tannie tried to smile. Butt purred against my ankles and pushed his bottom high in the air. I hugged Tannie for an extra long time.

I could tell by her face that Tannie still had some pain. I smiled a lot even though Tannie didn't look just like herself. Mom had told me to act happy so Tannie would see how glad we would be for her to come live with us. I didn't have to act one bit.

"Tannie, how are you?" Mom wanted to know.

"I'm all right for any old lady," she answered. She patted Mom's shoulder and held her cheek out for a kiss.

Mom kissed Tannie's cheek and held her close.

"How are you, really?" Mom asked again.

"Well, I'm not myself, if that's what you mean. I don't expect I will be for some time, if ever." Tannie paused and sighed. "I'm different,

Grace. I'll have to use a walker after this cast comes off. Everything is different now," Tannie told her.

Mom nodded like she understood. Butt licked his paws, then cleaned his face.

Tannie shooed us off to bed. "These girls have been on the road for too long, haven't they, Butt?" Butt looked up from his bath.

"Get some sleep," said Tannie. "We've plenty of time for catching up tomorrow."

But I couldn't sleep; neither could Mom. We were ready to talk Tannie into coming home with us.

In Tannie's big guest bed, where Mom and I slept, I whispered to Mom, "Are you sure she'll come? If I were Tannie, I wouldn't want to leave."

Butt hopped in the bed with us. He smushed the quilts down, turned around and around, and settled right on top of Mom's chest. Mom started to sneeze, "Tannie's a tough bird—*achoo*—that's for sure. We'll have some convincing to do, no doubt about it. *Achoo*."

I hoped Mom would do most of the convincing.

In the morning, Mom got up her courage while she made us pancakes and sausage for breakfast. Mom says it's easier to talk over a good meal.

I didn't go kick my soccer ball around the yard or race through the woods looking for quail. I didn't run to visit the chickens. I didn't hide in the low, tangled branches of Tannie's magnolia tree. I stayed right beside Mom while she told Tannie how we had everything ready for her in Virginia.

She asked Tannie nicely to come home with us, but that didn't work. Tannie didn't put up a big fuss at the idea of leaving the place she built with Saint Louis. She just didn't want to leave.

Tannie said, "Grace, if it's all the same to you, I'll stay here." Mom didn't give up. She's strong willed, too, just like Tannie and me.

Mom reminded Tannie of the time Tannie helped us, when we needed help the most. "When Michael and I split up? What did you do?"

Michael's my dad; he lives way across the country now. He's strong willed, too, just like the rest of us. Mom jokes that nobody ever called him Saint Michael. My dad lives in San Francisco — that's even farther from Virginia than Tannie's place.

Tannie looked at Mom and shook her head. "You girls are like my own, that's all."

Mom wasn't going to give in. "Tannie, you came to us then. You read Jenna stories and taught her every bird song you know."

"*Bob-white, bob-white,*" I whistled for special effect.

"That's good, Jenna. Do you remember the song of the eastern meadowlark?" Tannie asked.

"I would never forget it." And I sang the song of the eastern meadowlark for Tannie: *"Spring-of-the-year, spring-of-the-year."*

"How about the sweet little eastern towhee? Isn't he your favorite?"

"Drink-your-tea! Drink-your-teaaa!" I sounded just like the towhee.

"Ladies, stop changing the subject," Mom scolded us. "Tannie, the point is we're family. We need to be together."

Tannie wouldn't budge; Mom wouldn't quit.

"Aunt Britannia," Mom said softly, "we all need help sometimes."

Seven

It took a very lot of convincing and begging to get Tannie to agree. Tannie was running out of arguments. She tried to resist Mom one last time. She looked at Butt and patted her knees.

Butt jumped up in Tannie's lap and kneaded her pants with his tiny paws until his spot was just right for sleeping. Only Butt didn't fall asleep; I saw his little pink nose twitching, and his eyes were only pretending to be asleep. Butt was playing opossum!

"Well, what about Butt? Jenna, you love Butt, I know," Tannie said to me.

I rubbed my nose against Butt's nose to make him open his eyes.

Then Tannie looked at Mom. "You're allergic to cats, Grace. And I can't leave Butt." Tannie folded her arms like she thought she had won.

Butt is so smart; he jumped down from Tannie's lap and twisted himself around Mom's legs, meowing like he was a kitten. He's such a baby.

My mom loves Tannie so much that she picked Butt up in her arms and nuzzled his pink nose to hers. "I love Butt, too! We insist that Butt should come with you."

Tannie didn't say anything — she just got real quiet. I could tell she was thinking hard about it, but I didn't get too excited yet. I rubbed Butt's tummy until he started purring really loud like a lawn mower.

"Butt," I told him, "if you come to live with us, you can eat scraps from the kitchen and sleep in my room anytime you want. We even have a screened-in porch where you can stretch out in the sun all day long!"

I kissed Butt's nose again. Butt purred even louder.

After another minute, Tannie agreed. "Okay, girls. I will hate leaving this place. There are many, many memories of a wonderful life here. I suppose you're right. Butt and I will live with you. If that's what you really want."

With Butt still in her arms, Mom leaned over to Tannie and kissed her. "Yes! That's what we really want."

I gave Butt a tummy rub.

Then, Mom started to sneeze. *Achoo! Achoo! Achoo!*

"Must be all the pollen outside," said Mom. She set Butt down on the floor.

Eight

Tannie put her farm up for sale and her enormous pickup truck and her motorcycle, too. She gave the bossy rooster and the kind chickens to Mrs. Butler, who was in need of a rooster, anyhow. Tannie kissed each chicken on the head before we left. The movers put her sleigh bed and her piano in a trailer, and her grandfather clock and gardening tools, too.

Tannie and Mom sat in the front. Butt and I had the whole backseat to ourselves. Tannie would only stare out the front window. "I have to look ahead! I can't turn back," she said.

Mom sniffled and wiped her eyes. She reached her hand to Tannie's shoulder.

I watched out the window until we were gone, long down the road. The four of us drove back through the Great Smoky Mountains and the Blue Ridge Mountains, too, all the way home to our house in Virginia. Tannie rode the whole way with her good china in a box on her lap so it wouldn't break.

I had a feeling Tannie was right about everything being different now.

Tannie sure did seem different. I looked at my Tannie List, then put it away. My list would have to wait until Tannie got better. First, we had to learn fast how to help Tannie. Especially since she couldn't do everything by herself anymore. In fact, Tannie stopped doing most things for herself, because Mom did most things for her.

Mom cooked Tannie's meals and washed her clothes. She fixed Tannie's medicine and took Tannie to the doctor to cut off her cast. Mom even helped Tannie in the shower so she wouldn't slip and fall. Tannie hardly said a word. Something told me maybe she didn't like all of Mom's helping.

And when Mom brought home the new walker to help Tannie stay balanced, we learned that Tannie liked that even less.

"I have to take such extra care with simple things. I'm not supposed to bend over. I'm not supposed to squat down. I can't lift anything. I'm not used to this. I'm used to doing everything on my own," Tannie complained.

Mom tried to comfort her. "Your bones are so fragile that you have to be careful. Fragile bones take time to mend, you know, and it's best if they don't get broken at all. I'm going to take good care of you now; you don't have to worry about anything. Using your walker will help keep you safe," Mom said.

My special job was to keep track of Tannie's walker and remind her to use it all the time. Sometimes Tannie refused. If she walked down the hallway without it—holding on to doorknobs, teetering to the left, then tottering to the right—I would ask her, "Aunt Tannie, where is your walker?"

Tannie would just wave me off with her hand and a shrug. "I don't know. It's in the other room, I guess."

My other job was to keep Tannie's bird feeders filled. Even though we still hadn't put up any nest boxes, the eastern bluebirds perched on the power line every day. The northern cardinals kept watch on the fence gate. One day, I saw a bird I had never seen.

"What's that fuzzy-headed gray one?" I asked Tannie.

"That little tiny darling? That's called a phoebe!"

"A phoebe? There's a bird named after me? Jenna Phoebe?"

"Opposite. You are named after that fuzzy-headed bird!"

"Oh, it's so cute." I wished I could hold the phoebe in my hand.

"That was you on the day you were born, Jenna. So tiny and fuzzy and sweet, that I suggested that your parents give you that name."

"Aunt Tannie, is it time for me to start a life list?" I asked.

"I believe it is; I believe it is. That little eastern phoebe shall hold the most esteemed, number-one spot on your life list. You'll never forget that bird, even when you're old like me."

I think watching the birds with me was the most exciting part of Tannie's day. While Mom worked hard at the hospital and I worked hard at school, Tannie watched TV or read books or watched the birds at her window. But Tannie was used to more excitement. She was used to doing whatever she wanted to do. If you ask me, Tannie was getting bored in Virginia.

Poor Tannie. Would she ever have a big adventure again?

Nine

One day, when Mom and I came home, Tannie was nowhere to be found.

"Tannie? Tannie, where are you?" Mom hollered through the house.

"Butt?" I called in my room.

"Tannie, this isn't funny," Mom said to nobody.

"Butt! Butt! Baby-Butt!" I called under the sofa. Then I made a kissing sound; I walked all through the house; Butt did not come out.

I heard that mockingbird making a fuss outside. I ran to the back door.

"MOM!" I yelled. "I found Tannie's walker!" Mom came running.

"Uh-oh," she said. Mom threw open the screen door. The heat from outside rushed onto my face.

There was Tannie with one foot on a stepladder and one foot on the earth. She wasn't using her walker or being extra careful.

Tannie was about to climb the dogwood tree. Mom ran to Tannie, waving her arms in the air. "Stop! Stop! Do not climb up that tree!"

Tannie stepped back down, with both feet on the earth. She stood at attention and gave Mom a salute. I laughed out loud. Mom did not laugh.

Mom took a deep breath and then asked Tannie calmly, "What exactly are you doing out here? Why is there a ladder leaning on that tree?"

Tannie explained that it was no big deal.

She pointed toward the holly, where the mockingbird lived. "I wanted to see how many eggs might be in the nest."

Then Tannie looked up in the dogwood. "Butt came out with me, of course."

Butt cried from the tippy-top branches.

Tannie admitted, "You would think I'd know better than to stake out a mockingbird. That protective mama bird chased Butt right up the dogwood. I'm glad you're here. Grace, will you hold the ladder for me? The big baby won't come down."

Rescuing Butt sounded way fun to me! "I'll do it! I'll do it! I'll get Butt even without the stepladder!" I took off my socks and shoes and shimmied up the tree before Mom could tell me, "Do not climb up that tree!"

Tannie cheered me on. "That's it, Jenna! You're just the right size! Get on up that tree, little girl, and bring the big baby down to me!"

Butt cried louder: *MEOW! MEOW!*

Tannie was right; the dogwood was just my size for climbing. I reached Butt in a flash. He jumped safe into my arms, and we carefully climbed back down to Tannie and Mom.

Tannie shook my hand. "Jenna, you're a girl after my own heart."

"You're the one who taught me that the best way to climb a tree is barefooted," I said, giving Tannie the credit.

I looked at Mom, expecting her to tell me, "Good job, Jenna! You saved Butt's life."

Instead, she just said, "Ladies, let's go back inside before someone gets hurt." Mom looked at Tannie and took another deep breath. "Aunt Britannia, next time ask for help first. You could have really hurt yourself. I'm surprised you didn't lose your balance just moving the ladder."

"Grace, I've never needed much help," Tannie told Mom. "You know that."

Mom just said, "Tannie, come on. I'll help you with your shower after supper and after I pay the bills." Mom held Tannie's elbow tight going up the steps. Butt followed Tannie. I put the ladder away, all by myself, and made a note to add the mockingbird to my life list.

At bedtime, I waited to hear the mockingbird, but she didn't sing one note. I guessed she was too busy with her nest to sing. Butt curled up beside me and purred himself to sleep. I waited and waited for Mom. I reached under my pillow for my Tannie List. *Maybe tomorrow,* I thought, *I'll at least take care of number six. I'll win that soccer game for Tannie.*

Ten

This year, my spring soccer team was one of the best in the league. I was nervous about this first play-off game because it was the biggest game of my life. I was even more nervous because Tannie was coming to watch me and I wanted to win for her. Finally, I could do something on my Tannie List: Win a soccer game for Tannie!

In general, being the smallest girl on the field didn't make me nervous at all. Tannie always tells me, I might be little, but I'm fiery! I was definitely ready to be fiery on the field at my game for Tannie.

In the first half, I tore my uniform and skinned my knee, and then scored the only goal of the entire game. All of my teammates gave me high fives and whooped and hollered, "Yeah, Jenna!" I listened for Mom but didn't hear her shouting, "Jenna! Good job, Jenna!"

I tried to save my best jump header for when Mom and Tannie got there, but I had to use it anyway, because my team needed me. I closed my mouth, bent my knees, attacked that ball, and shot it over to my teammate!

"Nice pass, Jenna!" I heard Coach shout.

I kept looking out for Tannie and her walker, but I only ever saw a bunch of moms and dads and some baby strollers. Not one old lady showed up to watch my game, especially not the one I wanted to see.

After the game, Coach and I put away all the equipment. I hoped Mom would at least remember to pick me up.

I emptied out the water cooler. Did Mom forget me?

I helped the coach load up her car. Then we waited and waited some more. When Mom and Tannie finally got there, I was mad.

"You missed my goal! You missed it! This whole game was for Tannie." I hollered to keep from crying. Mom looked too tired to get after me for yelling. She shrugged. "Jenna, I had to take Tannie to the doctor. We're running a little late."

I looked over at Tannie, who had stayed in the car and was just sitting there in the front seat.

I stomped my foot. "This was the biggest, most important soccer game of my life!"

I looked over at Tannie again. She didn't even see me play. "It's not fair!" I shouted.

Tannie saw me and waved. I didn't feel like waving. I dropped my soccer ball and kicked it with all my might.

"Come on, Jenna. Don't be mad. Tannie needed me," Mom said.

Then I did start to cry. "Well, I needed somebody, too! I needed Tannie to see me win the game, just for her! I needed you to say, 'Good job, Jenna!' when I made a goal."

Mom pulled me in close, and even though I'm not a baby anymore, she picked me up in her arms.

"Good job, Jenna! Good job," she whispered in my ear.

I mashed my face into her neck and tried to plug my tears. "Do you love Aunt Britannia more than you love me?" I asked her.

Mom sighed. "Is that what you think?"

I hid again in Mom's neck and didn't say anything. Mom's earring tickled my cheek.

Mom held me tighter and said, "Tannie's our family, and I do love her. But, Jenna, you're my heart."

I twirled her earring around and around with my finger. "Hey, I gave you those earrings last Christmas," I said.

"I've been wearing them a lot lately. They're my very, very, very favorite pair. All my patients tell me how pretty they are. Then I always tell my patients all about you."

Just for a second, I pretended I was still really little and it was still just the two of us. I rested my head on Mom's shoulder. "I miss you, Mama," I said.

"I miss you, too. I know it's been hard and not much fun. We'll all get better at being a family; you'll see." I wiped away my tears and took Mom's hand. We walked back to the car together. Tannie waved even bigger when she saw me. I decided to wave back. And I hoped Mom was right.

Eleven

But things didn't get better.

They sort of got worse. One morning, when Mom and I were running late, we heard Tannie yelling.

"Girls! Girls! Girls!"

Then the walls started to shake.

BOOM-BOOM-BOOM!

That didn't sound like the school bus to me.

BOOM-BOOM-BOOM!

I called from my room, "Mom! Mom! Is it an earthquake?"

Mom came running out of her bedroom still in her pj's, looking sleepy and scared. She thought Tannie had fallen and was hurt on the stairs.

But there Tannie stood, at the bottom of the steps.

She was banging her walker against the wall.

"Girls, you're late! Get on down here, girls!"

BOOM-BOOM-BOOM!

Tannie kept right on banging that walker until we came down together.

When Mom marched downstairs, I knew Tannie was in big trouble, even though it was sort of nice of her to make us toast and juice for breakfast.

"Aunt Britannia! You are not our personal alarm clock! And your walker is NOT for banging—it's for walking!" Mom had never before bossed Tannie like that.

Tannie looked hurt and her voice got quiet.

"You have so much to do by yourself, Grace. I thought I would fix breakfast this morning. I didn't want you girls to be late—that's all."

Mom raised her eyebrows at Tannie. "I do not need you to put yourself in harm's way by doing crazy things with your walker. I don't need that kind of help."

Tannie looked at Mom for the longest time without saying a word. We all just stood there. I saw Butt's tail swishing under the sofa.

Finally, Tannie spoke. "Grace, we all need help sometimes."

After that, we all stayed quiet. Butt stayed under the sofa and wouldn't come out. I looked out the living-room window and wondered if I had missed the school bus yet. In the serviceberry bush outside the window, I spotted three brown birds with black masks and red-tipped wings.

"Look, Tannie! What are those birds? They're feeding each other!"

"Oh, Jenna! What a good eye you have for birds. That's the cedar waxwing. What a loving, gentle bird, one of my very favorites. Add the waxwing to your list right away!" I did add the waxwing to my life list. I watched the family of three waxwings take turns feeding one another berries. Would we ever learn to be loving and gentle like they were?

Twelve

I hoped it would be different, but that night as soon as we walked through the door, it was still like everybody had stopped even trying to learn to live together. Mom rushed to the kitchen so she could fix supper. Tannie started back to her room to watch TV. Butt and I played paper football on the floor.

Halfway down the hall, though, Tannie turned back and asked Mom, "Grace, do you need some help with supper?"

Mom answered, "No. I can do it myself. But thanks all the same."

Tannie stood there watching Mom until Mom looked up from chopping an onion.

"What?" Mom said in sort of a snippy way. "I said I can do it."

Then Mom tried to sound nicer. "You should go rest, Tannie. After supper and after I vacuum, I'll help you with your shower."

Tannie leaned on her walker and didn't say a word. She pushed her walker, one slow step at a time, all the way back down the hall and into the bathroom.

I heard Tannie start the shower. I looked at Mom.

Mom kept chopping onions; she must have heard it, too, but didn't look up.

I heard a big bang in the bathroom.

Mom dropped the knife and flew down the hall.

"Grace, all right, I could use some help," I heard Tannie call out, but pretty quietly.

"Tannie! Tannie, I'm coming!" Mom yelled. She dashed into the bathroom. Butt and I ran down the hall behind her.

I didn't expect to hear what I heard next.

Mom started laughing. "I'll say you could use some help. You're in a pickle, Tannie. Here, let me help. Oops. Oops. Oops. Come back, here." I heard an awful lot of banging. Had Mom dropped Tannie?

"Here, let me help you, Grace." The banging didn't stop. Had Tannie dropped Mom? The laughing didn't stop. What could be so funny?

I pushed the door open just to see for myself. I didn't knock.

There was Tannie in her birthday suit, sitting on her special shower chair. There Mom was right with her—apron, clothes, shoes, and all.

They both kept dropping the slippery soap.

Every time Mom almost caught the soap, it escaped like a game of keep-away.

Mom reached again for the soap. It shot out of her hand, hit the wall, and then landed in Tannie's lap. Tannie tried to grab it, and it slid right through her fingers. Tannie and Mom were laughing so hard, they were red in the face. Mom had to lean against the wall to keep from falling herself.

Tannie saw me in the doorway and said, "It's all right. You can stay in here with us. I lost my modesty a long time ago."

"That means Tannie's not shy, Jenna. Close the door, though, so Tannie doesn't get too cold."

So I got in the shower with all my clothes on, too, and scrubbed Tannie's back with a washcloth and washed her hair with a special shampoo for baby-fine hair.

Tannie washed her own legs. Mom says that Tannie still has the prettiest and strongest legs ever and that we are lucky that our legs are just like hers. Tannie says those are farm-girl legs and that they run in the family.

When we were all in the shower, dropping the soap, Butt meowed and meowed until we let him come in. Butt really is a big baby; he always cries when he gets left out. I don't blame him; I don't like to be left out either.

Thirteen

At supper, nobody was bossy and nobody was rude. Tannie said the blessing. Mom and Tannie closed their eyes and bowed their heads, while I tried to get Butt to bow his head, too. Tannie prayed:

"Thank You for everything!
For my fine family—Jenna and Grace.
For my true love—Louis.

For my new home, this good food, and my
dear old friend, Butt.
Thank You for everything! "

At exactly the very same second, Mom and I
added, "And thank you for Tannie!"

While we ate, Tannie said she wanted to call
a family meeting, something Mom and I had
never done before Tannie came. "There are two
rules to know about this, girls," Tannie told us.
"Number one: everybody gets to have their turn
to speak. Number two: everybody has to listen
when it's not their turn."

"My turn first," Tannie said. Mom giggled.
I picked Butt up in my lap because he had to
listen, too.

Tannie looked right at Mom said, "I need
to say something important. I want both you
girls to really listen. I've had a secret that I

haven't told anyone. Not even myself. I didn't know it until I came here, but I don't want to live alone anymore. You girls are like my own, and I want to be with you. We do need to change some things around here, though, if we're all to be happy."

Mom nodded, and I nodded, too. "You go first, Tannie. What would you like to change?" Mom asked her.

"Well, we could all be having a lot more fun together. My bones are fragile; I know that is a fact. I reckon I'll have to use this rotten walker forevermore. But there is still a lot left that I can do. If I can't dance the jitterbug anymore, I can still play a mean piano. I know I won't be kicking a soccer ball with Jenna ball anytime soon, but I can sit down in a chair and watch her win games."

Mom let Tannie keep on talking. "What else,

Tannie? What else needs to change around here?"

"I can help around here more than I do. I know I can't handle myself in the kitchen the way I did before this last fall. But I can surely teach you how to make pound cake. I probably shouldn't try to vacuum while I'm on the mend, but I can fold clothes until the cows come home; that's not going to hurt me."

Tannie grinned at Mom and reminded her, "Grace, we all need help sometimes."

Then Mom turned to me. "Jenna, how about you? What would you like to change around here?" Butt pawed my chin.

I pulled my Tannie List out of my back pocket. I looked at it hard before saying anything at all.

"Well," I started, "I agree with Tannie. We could have more fun, like we could build a tree house, dig a garden, or hang birdhouses. Maybe we could bake the pound cake tonight."

Mom nodded slowly. "Is there anything else?"

I looked at Tannie and smiled because I didn't want to hurt her feelings, but I had something even more important to say to Mom.

"Well," I started again, and then swallowed hard to make sure that I said it right. "I mean, you haven't tucked me in once since Tannie moved here."

"Really?" Mom blinked and cocked her head. "Oh, Jenna."

Mom got up from her chair and came to squat down by me. "I guess I have been so busy trying to take care of everything after work. Have I been taking care of everything but you?"

I didn't answer.

Thankfully, Tannie spoke up. "What a good family meeting this has been! We know what

I need—more fun. We know what Jenna needs—more fun, and more of her mother."

I remembered the first family meeting rule. "Mom, now it's your turn to talk."

Mom thought for a minute. "The same, I suppose. I need more fun. I need you and Tannie to forgive me for being so bossy lately. And, I guess—I guess I do need some help around here, too. There, I asked for help."

We all cleaned up after supper together, instead of Mom doing it all by herself.

Butt paced around the floor, flipping his pretty tail around, begging for scraps.

Tannie threw him a potato slice, and he ate it! Mom threw him a broccoli flower, and he ate it!

Tannie joked, "Butt, are you a vegetarian as well as a pacifist?"

Butt looked up at her and answered, *Meow.*

"Well, you learn something new every day."

We all laughed.

We made our first pound cake together and then straightened up the house while it baked. Tannie and I sat in the dining room and folded clothes while Mom ran the vacuum. Butt hid behind the couch and pounced at Mom's shoe when she came around the corner.

When Tannie's grandfather clock started its eight o'clock bedtime chimes, I kissed Tannie good night, and she told me, "Sleep sweet, little Phoebe!"

Mom tucked Butt and me into my bed and read to us for a long, long time. She didn't rush off to do chores or take care of Tannie. She cuddled up next to me and rested her eyes. We could hear Tannie downstairs playing a sleepy-sounding "Church Bells Do Chime" on the piano.

"That sounds nice," I said. Butt curled up by me and kneaded a just-right spot on my Sunbonnet Sue quilt. Mom whispered, "Tannie's right, Jenna Phoebe: being a family is supposed to be fun."

I sat straight up. "I forgot something," I blurted out.

Mom reached for the lamp. Butt stood up, stretched his pretty paws, and swished his tail high in the air.

"Sorry, Butt," I said. "Will you hand me my Tannie List, Mama? And a pencil, too?"

I unfolded the paper and reread one through six.

I realized I had left out the most important one of all.

Number 7: Remember to ask for help sometimes, I wrote.

"That's better." I gave the list and the pencil back to Mom. "I added seven for a secret never to be told."

She read my words and clutched the paper to her heart. "Not so secret anymore. I'll make this my number seven, too! That way I won't ever forget again."

Mom kissed my nose and turned out the light.

The mama mockingbird perched outside my window decided my bedtime was just the right time for singing. I didn't dream of Tannie or Butt or Mama. Or of roosters or chickens or soccer. I dreamed of fortune-telling crows and cedar waxwings, all loving and helping one another.

AFTER TANNIE COMES

1. Build a tree house.
2. Dig a garden.
3. Hang bluebird boxes.
4. ~~Make a cozy place for Butt in my room.~~
5. ~~Bake pound cake every day.~~
6. ~~Win a soccer game for Tannie.~~
7. ~~Remember to ask for help sometimes.~~

Dear Reader,

I bet you have a special older person in your life. Your Nana or your Dado? Or another elder, who lives in your building or on your street? A wise friend once told me, "Elders are superheroes." I agree! If elders are superheroes, that means they have superpowers, right?

Just like Tannie in the book, my grandparents had the superpower of knowing all about birds. I first learned to identify backyard birds from my grandmothers, who often pointed out the flashy blue of a jay, the fiery red of a male cardinal, or the telltale tail-flick of a mockingbird. My granddaddy taught me to whistle the call of the quail: "Bob-white. Bob-bob white." Even now, these birds remind me of my grandparents and of my childhood in Mississippi.

Counting crows is a game that my father learned from his mother, and he taught me. The tradition actually started hundreds of years ago with a British nursery rhyme about magpies called "One for Sorrow." Whenever I see a murder of crows (that's what you call a bunch of crows hanging out together), I still count them the same way Jenna does.

Crows, you may know, are very smart birds. They can use their beaks to hammer and crack. They form tight-knit communities to protect and help one another. And scientists have proven that crows recognize the humans who share their space!

If you'd like to develop a bird-loving superpower of your own, here are some ideas to get started:

• The next time you visit a beloved older person, ask him or her to tell you a story about the birds of their childhood. Then you could share a story about the birds you've encountered.

• Compare life lists with an elder. (What? You haven't started yours yet? You can begin right now! Chances are that wherever you are, whatever the time of day, no matter the weather, there's a bird outside that you can hear or see.)

• Learn new words from birds. Some of my favorite bird words are *clutch, perch, fledging,* and *cavity* (the kind in a tree, not in your mouth).

Happy birding, and let me know what you see and hear!

Love,
Gigi